BIG BEND

BIG BEND

NATIONAL PARK

NATE FRISCH

CREATIVE EDUCATION · CREATIVE PAPERBACKS

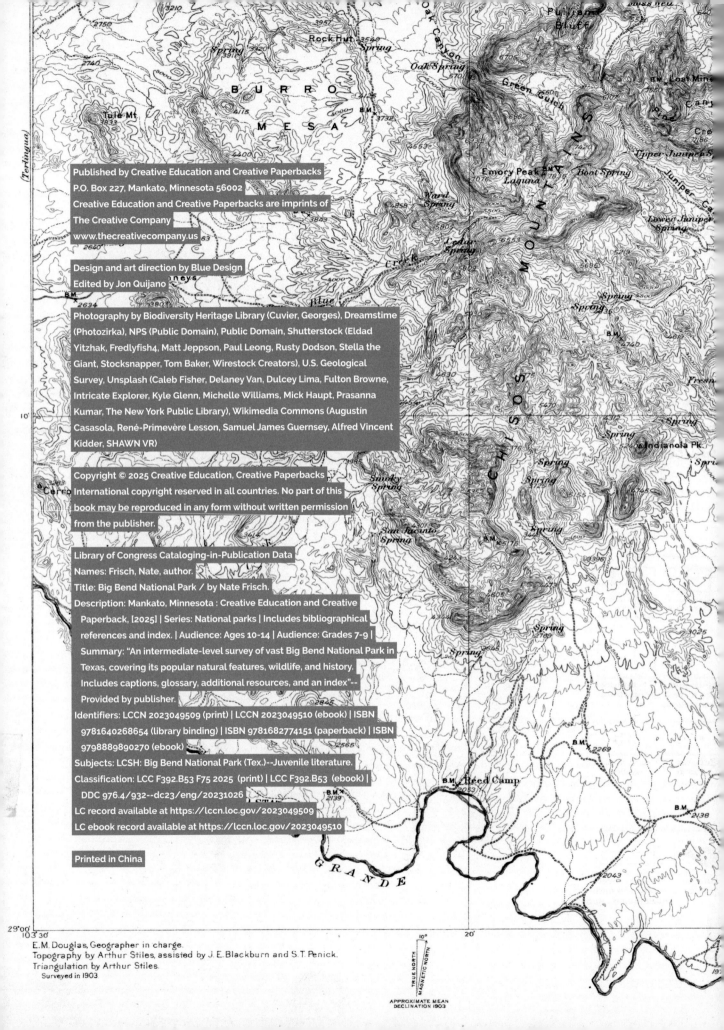

Published by Creative Education and Creative Paperbacks
P.O. Box 227, Mankato, Minnesota 56002
Creative Education and Creative Paperbacks are imprints of
The Creative Company
www.thecreativecompany.us

Design and art direction by Blue Design
Edited by Jon Quijano

Photography by Biodiversity Heritage Library (Cuvier, Georges), Dreamstime (Photozirka), NPS (Public Domain), Public Domain, Shutterstock (Eldad Yitzhak, Fredlyfish4, Matt Jeppson, Paul Leong, Rusty Dodson, Stella the Giant, Stocksnapper, Tom Baker, Wirestock Creators), U.S. Geological Survey, Unsplash (Caleb Fisher, Delaney Van, Dulcey Lima, Fulton Browne, Intricate Explorer, Kyle Glenn, Michelle Williams, Mick Haupt, Prasanna Kumar, The New York Public Library), Wikimedia Commons (Augustin Casasola, René-Primevère Lesson, Samuel James Guernsey, Alfred Vincent Kidder, SHAWN VR)

Library of Congress Cataloging-in-Publication Data
Names: Frisch, Nate, author.
Title: Big Bend National Park / by Nate Frisch.
Description: Mankato, Minnesota : Creative Education and Creative Paperback, [2025] | Series: National parks | Includes bibliographical references and index. | Audience: Ages 10-14 | Audience: Grades 7-9 | Summary: "An intermediate-level survey of vast Big Bend National Park in Texas, covering its popular natural features, wildlife, and history. Includes captions, glossary, additional resources, and an index"-- Provided by publisher.
Identifiers: LCCN 2023049509 (print) | LCCN 2023049510 (ebook) | ISBN 9781640268654 (library binding) | ISBN 9781682774151 (paperback) | ISBN 9798889890270 (ebook)
Subjects: LCSH: Big Bend National Park (Tex.)--Juvenile literature.
Classification: LCC F392.B53 F75 2025 (print) | LCC F392.B53 (ebook) | DDC 976.4/932--dc23/eng/20231026
LC record available at https://lccn.loc.gov/2023049509
LC ebook record available at https://lccn.loc.gov/2023049510

Printed in China

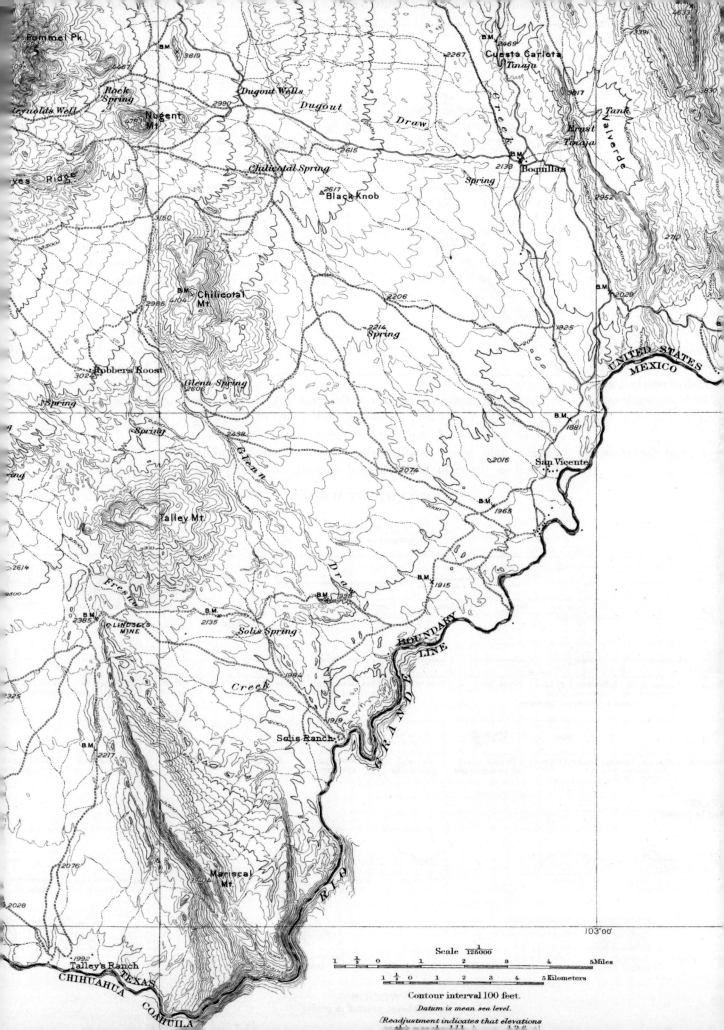

Pummel Pk

B.M. × 3619

Rock Spring

Reynolds Well

Nugent Mt 4763

Dugout Wells

2990

Dugout

Draw

B.M. 2469

Cuesta Carlota
Tinaja

2267

3017

Creek

Tank

Valverde

2615

Ernst
Tinaja

Chilicotal Spring

Boquillas
B.M.
2138

Spring

3391

3330

2952

2617
Black Knob

yes Ridge

3150

2710

3500

B.M. × 2986 × 4104 Chilicotal Mt

2206

2029 B.M.

2214
Spring

1925

Robbers Roost

3024

UNITED STATES

Spring

Glenn Spring
2606

MEXICO

Spring

2458

1881 B.M.

Spring

2074

2016

San Vicente

Talley Mt

2000

3000

Glenn

B.M.
1965

2614

3500

Draw

B.M. × 1915

2500

Fresno

B.M. × 2385

LINDSEY'S
MINE

B.M.
2135

B.M. 1999

2076

Solis Spring

1984

Creek

2076

2028

1919

2000

Solis Ranch

RIO

BOUNDARY LINE

GRANDE

B.M. × 2217

2325

2076

Mariscal
Mt

RIO

Talley's Ranch
1992

CHIHUAHUA

TEXAS

COAHUILA

103°00'

CONTENTS

Towering mountains and glassy lakes. Churning rivers and dense forests. Lush prairies and blistering deserts. The open spaces and natural wonders of the United States once seemed as limitless as they were diverse. But as human expansion and development increased in the 1800s, forests and prairies were replaced by settlements and agricultural lands. Waterways were diverted, wildlife was overhunted, and the earth was scarred by mining. Fortunately, many Americans fought to preserve some of the country's vanishing wilderness. In 1872, Yellowstone National Park was established, becoming the first true national park in the world and paving the way for future preservation efforts. In 1901, Theodore Roosevelt became U.S. president. He once stated, "There can be no greater issue than that of conservation in this country." During his presidency, Roosevelt signed five national parks into existence. The National Park Service (NPS) was created in 1916 to manage the growing number of U.S. parks. In 1944, Big Bend National Park in southwestern Texas joined that list. The park has been largely overlooked in the decades since, but its dynamic blend of geological, biological, and cultural history has captured the interest and affections of those who've ventured into the remote desert region.

BIG BEND NATIONAL PARK

Located far from any major city, Big Bend National Park is separated from Mexico by the curving Rio Grande.

Volcanic activity helped shape rock formations in Big Bend National Park.

An Ever-Changing Landscape

Big Bend National Park lies within the Chihuahuan Desert, the largest desert in North America. Although the term "desert" often conjures up images of rocky, sun-baked earth, Big Bend is a vibrant region with a rich geological history of diverse landscapes and **ecosystems**. Some of the oldest rock layers, or strata, in the area date back 500 million years. Around that time, deep ocean waters covered most of what is now Texas.

About 300 million years ago, **tectonic** plates to the south shifted north. The collision filled in what had previously been ocean and created the Ouachita Mountains. The range stretched all the way to the Appalachian Mountains of the eastern U.S. and extended down into southwestern Texas. The Ouachitas may have been as high as today's Rocky Mountains, but over the millennia, **erosion** has worn the soft rock of the range down to the point that it is barely noticeable in Texas anymore.

Although the peaks basically vanished, the overall elevation of the region remained higher, and when the Big Bend area went back underwater 135 million years ago, it became a shallow tropical sea. Layers of mud and sand accumulated on the seafloor, as did the calcium-rich shells and bones of ancient fish, shellfish, and snails.   When the sea began receding 100 million years ago, the layers of deposited sediments and minerals solidified into **sedimentary rock**. Mud became shale, sand became sandstone, and bone and shell deposits became limestone. Trapped within these rock layers were the fossils of giant clams, oysters, fish, and marine reptiles. Fossils of turtles and crocodiles in newer strata indicate a transition from seas to swamps. Dinosaur remains in still younger strata coincided with increasingly drier habitats.

Around 80 million years ago, the uplift of other mountain ranges began. Opposing forces within the earth created a break, or fault, that ran from what is now northern Canada all the way down to Mexico. In the north, the Rocky Mountains were formed. Around the same time, the Sierra Madres of Mexico rose up. Both extended into the Big Bend region, but again the soft, sedimentary rock became worn down, making the present-day peaks a fraction of their original size. Still, the 3,932-foot (1,198 meters) Mariscal Mountain in Big Bend serves as a reminder of the Texas Rockies, and the low Sierra del Carmen mountains—plus the Sierra del Caballo Muerto range within them—still stand at the eastern edge of the region. As those mountains eroded, new layers of sandstone built up. Within them is fossil evidence of prehistoric camels, horses, and rhinoceroses. Some plants and trees were also preserved and proved that the area was more heavily vegetated than it is today.

Around 38 to 32 million years ago, Big Bend got its own mountain range as a result of volcanic activity. As heat and pressure built up within the earth, molten rock, or magma, was forced upward. The

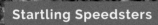

Startling Speedsters

Red racers or western coachwhips—either moniker is appropriate for the speedy, brightly colored, slender snakes. Young red racers typically have duller brown or gray coloration that shifts to pink or red as they grow to be six feet (1.8 m) in length. They are non-venomous, non-constricting snakes and feed only on small reptiles, rodents, birds, eggs, and insects. But they will respond aggressively if approached too closely and can slither faster than most humans jog. Coachwhips can frequently be seen basking in the desert sun, but they are also at home among shaded tree branches and even in water.

magma pressed against the rock layers above. In some cases, the magma broke completely through the sedimentary layers, and lava oozed out and cooled, resulting in ever-heightening layers of volcanic rock. In this way, the isolated Chisos Mountains were formed. Because the range is made of more resilient igneous stone, it is likely to last longer than previous mountains in the area, and its tallest summit, Emory Peak, measures 7,825 feet (2,385 m) high.

In other parts of Big Bend, upwelling magma fractured or melted sedimentary strata, but instead of pushing above ground, the molten rock simply filled in gaps beneath the surface. The magma then solidified into rigid stone. The surrounding sedimentary rock has since eroded away to reveal steep igneous formations, such as Casa Grande, Maverick Mountain, and the Mule Ears.

Today, active hot springs hint at the region's volcanic past. Hot springs are places where water is naturally heated underground and then pools at the earth's surface. Warmer groundwater constantly rises to replace the liquid that cools at the surface, and the Langford Hot

Springs in Big Bend maintain a temperature of 105 °Fahrenheit (40.6 °Celsius) throughout the year.

After the volcanic activity subsided, other geologic forces continued reshaping the region. Starting around 25 million years ago, violent earthquakes were common along a fault that stretched from the West Coast to Big Bend. Landmasses on opposing sides of the faults separated and became misaligned, and rock layers that were once connected sit as much as 4,800 feet (1,463) apart in elevation today.

The combination of elevation inequality, varying rock hardness, and an **arid** climate makes canyon formation a more likely event. Because rainfall is rare and the soil is dry, a sudden downpour will sweep away any loose sediment. When the land was flatter, water would run to lower ground in broad, thin sheets. But over time, small trenches formed where sediment was loosest, and later, rainwater would course along with increased force. Eventually, water became channeled into a few erosive routes that continued to carve the landscape. And no route in the area is more powerful than the Rio Grande.

The Rio Grande River begins in Colorado, runs through New Mexico, and forms the natural border between Texas and Mexico before emptying into the Gulf of Mexico. Although the river runs almost entirely south or southeast, it curves and flows northeast for about 100 miles (161 kilometers) at one point. This change of course accounts for the region's "Big Bend" label. Along this bend, the Rio Grande has carved out the Santa Elena Canyon, which features sheer cliff walls up to 1,500 feet (457) high.

Desert Opportunists

Javelinas, also called collared peccaries, look a lot like their relatives, the pigs. And like pigs, they are hearty and agreeable eaters. They particularly like prickly pear cactus, a source of both food and moisture. Weighing up to 55 pounds (25 kilograms) and bearing short and straight turks, javelinas can be dangerous prey for any black bears, mountain lions, or coyotes that target them. If a herd—which can range from 5 to 30 individuals—is threatened, javelinas make woofing sounds or pop their jaws together. When herds flee from danger, they do so in a wild jailbreak, scattering in all directions.

PARK
2
FACTS

Home to the entire Chisos Mountain range, Big Bend National Park includes both desert and mountain vistas.

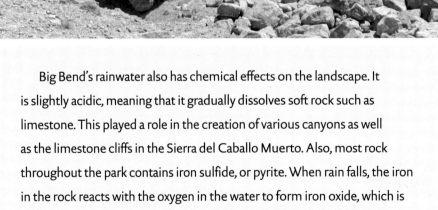

Engine-Powered Horses

Although various **concessionaires** offer guided river trips and SUV tours in and around Big Bend, many visitors are surprised that the Texas-based park has no horseback-riding outfitters. But in recent years, a different type of personal mount has been offered—an ATV. The four-wheelers accommodate one or two riders, and after a quick lesson on safe operation of the vehicle, guests follow a tour guide along the park's western border. Such a tour has multiple benefits, including access to areas that many automobiles are unable to navigate, learning regional information from the guides, and simply having fun driving the nimble vehicles.

Big Bend's rainwater also has chemical effects on the landscape. It is slightly acidic, meaning that it gradually dissolves soft rock such as limestone. This played a role in the creation of various canyons as well as the limestone cliffs in the Sierra del Caballo Muerto. Also, most rock throughout the park contains iron sulfide, or pyrite. When rain falls, the iron in the rock reacts with the oxygen in the water to form iron oxide, which is rust. This accounts for the warm, reddish hue seen throughout the region.

Rainfall, along with temperature, also plays a defining role in Big Bend's ecosystems. Areas at lower elevations have temperatures that regularly exceed 100 °F (37.8 °C) on summer days and receive only about

Catfish

10 inches (25.4 centimeters) of rain annually. In the Chisos Mountains, though, temperatures are often 20 °F (11.1 °C) cooler, and rainfall totals are almost double.

The drier, lower areas feature many types of **succulents** such as prickly pear cacti, agaves, and sotol. Up in the Chisos Mountains, junipers, oaks, pines, and aspens make up a rare forested oasis amid the desert. Back down below, springs and riverbanks support leafy trees, including cottonwoods and willows. Mesquite trees often inhabit the transitional zones between moist and dry areas, and patches of grassland are found on the lower slopes of the Chisos.

Collared lizard

Invertebrates (animals without backbones) such as scorpions and tarantulas inhabit the desert, as do many reptiles, including rattlesnakes, western coachwhips, banded geckos, and collared lizards. Big Bend is home to 20 species of bats, including the endangered Mexican long-nosed bat. Larger mammals such as black bears, mountain lions, and deer prefer the forested mountains, and javelinas and coyotes thrive almost anywhere. Various birds migrate to or through the region as the seasons change. More than 450 bird species have been identified in the area, including numerous songbirds, hummingbirds, woodpeckers, roadrunners, and **raptors**. The Rio Grande and a couple of its **tributaries** contain catfish, but other fish in the area are tiny, such as the Big Bend gambusia, which is found in a single hot-spring pond.

The Comanche and other western tribes became horse experts, using the animals to better hunt big game and battle enemies.

Many Owners, Many Uses

Atlatl

Although Big Bend may look like a poor place for humans to live, the region has been home to many different peoples over the years. Around 10,000 years ago, the area was cooler and wetter than it is now and supported more vegetation and large animals such as bison. At this time, **nomadic** Paleo-Indians followed and hunted these large animals with crude spears.

As the climate warmed up, much of the plant and animal life vanished from the area. Most of the people moved toward the Rio Grande, where plants were more abundant and animals came to feed and drink. These somewhat permanent residents are called Archaic Indians, and they employed dart-throwing devices known as atlatls for hunting smaller, faster game.

Artifacts from 1,000 years ago give evidence of early farming practices. Worn into rock, round holes called mortar holes or metates show where crops such as maize were ground into meal by using stone hand tools called pestles. The bow and arrow also replaced atlatls during this time.

The specific names of Native American tribes are typically known only as far back as the 1500s, when visiting Spaniards began documenting their communities. Alvar Nuñez Cabeza de Vaca led the first European expedition near Big Bend, passing by on the south side of the Rio Grande and encountering Chisos Native Americans in the region. More Spanish conquistadors (the Spanish word for conquerors) would follow. They sought gold, tried to convert natives to Christianity, took Native Americans as slaves, and claimed huge areas of land (including Big Bend) as "New Spain." They also changed Native American life by bringing horses to the New World, which allowed tribes to travel, hunt, and fight differently from before.

Alvar Nuñez Cabeza de Vaca

Eventually, Mescalero Apaches moved into the Big Bend region and forced the Chisos out. The Apaches, in turn, were driven off by Comanche from the north, who often conducted nighttime raids down to the Rio Grande and beyond, taking captives, supplies, and horses. The Comanche ransomed captives back to their families or tribes, sold them to Spaniards, or adopted them into their own bands. Although the Spaniards built some forts in the area, it was mostly the Comanche who held sway in Big Bend well into the 17th century.

Back in Europe in the early 1800s, French emperor Napoleon I waged war against neighboring countries, including Spain. As Spain focused its military efforts on France, its outposts in the New World were spread thin. Mexico declared its independence from Spain in 1810 and won the resulting war by 1821, when all of New Spain came under Mexican control. This area included present-day Mexico as well as Texas and the lands that would become California, Arizona, Nevada, Utah, New Mexico, and Oklahoma.

The Comanche still carried out raids in Texas at the time. To help curb the attacks, Mexico encouraged American settlers to come to the sparsely populated area. By the 1830s, Texas contained more American immigrants than Mexicans, and they started taking control of their own government rather than abiding by Mexican laws. In response, Mexico sent a military force to Texas. This prompted American Texans to declare their independence from Mexico in 1836. For a decade, Texas operated as an independent nation, but conflict with Mexico continued. When Texas agreed to become part of the U.S. in 1846, bitterness erupted into the Mexican-American War.

During the war, the U.S. fought to hold on to Texas but also wanted to add Mexican lands farther west. When the conflict ended in 1848, the U.S. retained Texas and claimed 500,000 square miles (1,294,994 sq km) of land that became the American Southwest. Mexico was given $15 million as compensation, and the border between the nations remained open for the most part.

Mexican ranchers who'd grazed their livestock in Big Bend before the war continued to do so afterward. American ranchers and settlers joined them later in the 1800s, especially after the Southern Pacific Railroad was extended through south Texas. Big Bend had more grasslands at that time, and for a couple decades, cattle, sheep, and goats grazed heavily. Because the grass was consumed faster than it could grow back, by 1900, fewer areas remained suitable for ranching.

Around the same time that many ranchers were seeking greener pastures, tourism was starting to grow. Perhaps the first promoted attraction was J. O. Langford's hot springs. As a child, Langford had battled the disease malaria, which had left him with ongoing health complications. Later, Langford heard that hot springs in Big Bend could

23

cure any ailment. So in 1909, he staked a claim on the land containing the hot springs and soaked in and drank from them on a daily basis. After his health improved, he advertised the curative properties of the springs and charged visitors a small fee to enter the bathhouse he constructed there. Whether they cured illness or not, the hot springs grew in popularity, and visitors who came for the springs were also impressed by the region's diverse scenery.

Farming and mercury mining also expanded in Big Bend during the early 1900s, and the villages of Castolon, Terlingua, and Boquillas arose near the Rio Grande. Mariscal Mine on Mariscal Mountain was among the more successful mines and supported a rare, non-riverside settlement. An area called Glenn Springs featured cool springs and was popular for ranching and farming. In 1914, a factory built near the springs relied on the water source and locally growing candelilla plants for the production of wax. Stores and trading posts sprang up to accommodate the factory workers, farmers, and ranchers.

Beginning the Day at Night

For a unique Big Bend experience, campers might start their day a couple hours before sunup. This dark and silent time is ideal for appreciating the night sky. After stargazing a while, a slow drive or walk with flashlights along desert roads will provide good opportunities to spot animals such as coyotes, javelinas, and snakes that tend to be active before and at daybreak. The nighttime animal search will give way to a sunrise over the Sierra del Caballo Muertos. Early risers east of the Chisos Mountains can be rewarded with impressive sunlight reflections off the rocky slopes.

PARK **4** FACTS

Natural Spring Paradise

Driving a little more than two hours north of Big Bend takes visitors to Balmorhea State Park. The park is small but boasts the world's largest spring-fed swimming pool. The edges of the 1.75-acre (0.7 ha) pool were artificially shaped by the Civilian Conservation Corps (CCC) in the 1930s, but beneath the surface is a natural rocky bottom that descends as far as 25 feet (7.6 m). The San Solomon Springs continuously pump cool, clear water into the pool, which then feeds into nearby wetlands via canals, and various rare fish species share the pool with swimmers, snorkelers, and scuba divers.

PARK 5 FACTS

The Mexican Revolution of the 1910s prompted many Mexicans to travel north to work at places such as the wax factory. Unfortunately, Mexican bandits came up as well to steal food and supplies from small settlements. In 1916, a raid on Glenn Springs left several villagers dead or injured, and buildings were burned to the ground. Afterward, U.S. military camps were set up at Glenn Springs, Castolon, and other villages along the Rio Grande. The army left four years later when the Mexican Revolution and border raids had ended.

By then, the wax business had faded away, and most ranchers and farmers had departed, making Glenn Springs a ghost town. Castolon, on the other hand, incorporated military buildings into the village, using them as stores, trading posts, or storage facilities for crops and farming

*Emiliano Zapata,
Mexican revolutionary*

equipment. As businesses and the population increased in Castolon, a couple named Elmo and Ada Johnson decided to establish an isolated trading post and ranch downriver in 1927.

Unfortunately, a brief Mexican revolt in 1929 resulted in more banditry, and the Johnsons' trading post was looted and their livestock driven away. The U.S. military returned, this time setting up an air force base on the Johnson ranch that would operate into the 1940s. Despite the military presence, some Americans living in the region took the law into their own hands, killing Mexicans suspected of being bandits. Decades of violence and looting and hit-and-miss business ventures were wearing thin with residents, and as more of them left Big Bend, abandoned ranches, farmsteads, and mines were added to the ruins of old Spanish forts in the region.

But appreciation for the natural landscape had quietly remained. In 1932, that admiration gained a humble but determined voice in the form of Texas state representative Everett Townsend. Townsend had spent the previous 40 years working as a frontier lawman and rancher in and around the Big Bend region. A trip into the Chisos Mountains as a young man had a profound effect on Townsend, and for decades, he'd thought of ways to preserve the land.

As a new politician from a scarcely populated region, Townsend doubted his own influence in the state senate, but, along with Abilene senator Robert Wagstaff, he wrote and submitted a bill to create Texas Canyons State Park around the Chisos. The bill was approved in 1933, and continued efforts resulted in a park expansion just months later. With the expansion came a new name—Big Bend State Park.

Rustic Beginnings and New Challenges

Although the park was authorized in 1933, much work remained to be done to make the area fully functional. A large portion of the land was still owned by ranchers, even though it wasn't good for grazing. The state of Texas began raising and allocating funds to buy up the private property within proposed park boundaries. As land was attained, it then needed to be made accessible to visitors.

Much of the park's early development was done by the Civilian Conservation Corps (CCC). The CCC was a work relief program initiated by president Franklin D. Roosevelt during the Great Depression, when years of drought and economic hard times left many people poor and unemployed. The program was supervised by the U.S. Army, which hired young single men and assigned them to manual labor and conservation tasks throughout public lands.

Townsend was instrumental in getting 200 CCC workers—many of Mexican descent—assigned to Big Bend State Park in 1934. However, the area lacked a consistent water source, and many places where water was available were still privately owned. Townsend himself led a small expedition in the Chisos Mountains and found a suitable water supply for a CCC base camp. The CCC set up tents and, later, barracks in the Chisos Mountains Basin. Among the first projects they tackled was the

Containing abandoned mines and other structures, ghost towns have become a popular Big Bend tourist stop.

development of a road in this mountainous area—a task completed mostly with hand tools.

The would-be state park made good progress early on, but Townsend felt the region was worthy of the more prestigious designation of a national park. Others supported this idea, and in 1935, both the state and federal government agreed that the park could eventually be taken over by the NPS. Big Bend would remain under Texas's control until the park was ready for visitors, and the state ultimately bought up more than 900 square miles (2,331 sq km) of private land within the park. The CCC would go on to construct park stores and lodges and groom numerous trails.

Plans for further development were in the works, but America's entry into World War II effectively put an end to the CCC in 1942. Sixteen million Americans, including most of the CCC workers, volunteered for or were drafted into the military. Nonetheless, the CCC's prior efforts were sufficient enough that on June 12, 1944, Roosevelt officially established Big Bend National Park. The 1,250-square-mile (3,237 sq km) park featured 118 miles (190 km) of the Rio Grande as its southern border, while the artificial boundaries to the north were constrained by private lands. The former CCC barracks became the park headquarters. This and other CCC-era buildings are still used today, as is the old Basin Road route.

World War II also led to another chapter in the hot-and-cold relationship between the U.S. and Mexico. Before the war, restrictions were in place to limit Mexican immigration. However, in order for U.S. farms, railways, and construction projects in the U.S. to continue operating while Americans fought overseas, the two nations agreed to a temporary lifting of the restrictions, and millions of migrant workers were recruited into the U.S.

Meanwhile, Oklahoman geologist Ross Maxwell was chosen to be Big Bend's first superintendent. He had a staff of only four, including a disgruntled NPS-appointed ranger who equated the desert region to hell. The park had no phones, electricity, or paved roads. During Maxwell's eight-year tenure, he oversaw several modern upgrades and carefully planned out a road that highlighted numerous formations, overlooks, and a stretch of the Santa Elena Canyon. That road is now known as the Ross Maxwell Scenic Drive.

While the park was making strides in providing visitor amenities, the region was suffering setbacks in wildlife preservation. Black bears and bighorn sheep had inhabited various low mountain ranges in and around Big Bend when ranchers had first moved in. But the livestock transmitted diseases to the native bighorns, and the sheep and bears were shot by hunters for their meat, hides, and horns. Bears were also killed because they were thought to be a threat to livestock. Populations steadily shrank

Black bear

until the bears were gone in the 1940s. The bighorns followed soon after. Human activity also drove away Atlantic sturgeon and American eel in the 1950s. Both fish had resided in Big Bend's Rio Grande during certain times of the year, but the building of dams downriver prevented the fish from traveling to and from their spawning grounds in the Gulf of Mexico.

The migrant labor arrangement between the U.S. and Mexico ended in 1964, when Congress determined that the Mexican workers who had been beneficial during the war were now taking too many jobs from the American workforce. However, many Mexicans wanted to continue working in the U.S. Some who were not authorized to enter the country would sneak in through isolated border regions such as Big Bend.

In the decades since, illegal immigration has been a hot-button topic in the U.S., and the U.S.-Mexico border is patrolled to discourage unlawful crossings. This monitoring includes Big Bend, and it presents some hazy legal situations in the park. Among them is using watercraft on the Rio Grande. The actual border between the nations lies unseen in the river, but the river itself is considered to be shared international territory. As of 2014, Rio Grande boaters do not need a passport to be anywhere on the water, but debarking on the opposite riverbank is illegal.

Some people do illegally enter Big Bend from Mexico, but these are mostly vendors trying to sell crafts, regional artifacts, or other souvenirs to tourists. However harmless their intentions, their behavior is outlawed, and knowingly buying from such vendors is also prohibited. To alleviate this issue, Big Bend park staff legally acquire some art and craftwork made across the Rio Grande and sell them in park shops, thus enabling the artists to make money and tourists to have safe access to the products.

Human crossing of the Rio Grande river is restricted, but black bears also cross the river. They wandered up from Mexico and reinhabited the

The scenic views, varying rapids, and towering rock walls make Big Bend popular for river trips.

A Desert Oasis

About 200 miles (322 km) east of Big Bend lies Amistad National Recreation Area. The focal point here is the International Amistad Reservoir, which was made by the damming of the Rio Grande. The 100 square miles (259 sq km) of water offer unexpected scenery and activities in the middle of the desert. Fishing is especially popular, and televised bass tournaments are held annually. Watercraft ranging from kayaks to jet skis to houseboats are used as well, and waterskiing, swimming, and scuba diving are common pastimes. On shore, picnic areas, hiking trails, and campgrounds are available to visitors.

Chisos in the late 1980s. Although their numbers have remained small to this day, enough bears live in the region to reproduce and sustain a modest population.

Bighorn sheep began their comeback several years later. Unlike the bears, they were reintroduced through human efforts. Over the past couple decades, bighorns have been released in Big Bend's Sierra del Caballo Muerto range, as well as in Black Gap Wildlife Management Area to the northwest, the Sierra del Carmen range in Mexico, and Big Bend Ranch State Park to the west. Bighorn sightings in Big Bend remain rare, but the clusters of protected areas offer promising habitat.

The arrival of other life forms in the park has been only too successful. Prominent among them is the tamarisk, or salt cedar—a tree from Africa and Eurasia that thrives in harsh environments. In the early 1900s, the trees were purposely introduced into many arid regions in the U.S. to control erosion and provide windbreaks. However, tamarisks' salty leaves ruin soil for other plants. They also absorb large amounts of water, leaving little for anything else. Worst of all, their seeds spread and take hold rapidly. Managing these invasive plants is a constant battle in Big Bend.

While tamarisks threaten the park's landscapes, human activity has tainted the Rio Grande. As more factories, farms, and homes have been built along the river, more waste and agricultural runoff have entered its waters. Since the 1990s, the river has contained unhealthy amounts of microbes and chemicals. Since this water flows from upstream, there is little that can be done within the park to remedy the problem. It is a reminder that preservation, or lack thereof, extends beyond any single location.

The park has been described as a "paradise" for scientists and nature explorers on the hunt for fossils and other remains.

An Enormous Hidden Gem

n recent years, Big Bend National Park has received about 400,000 visitors annually. By comparison, other western parks such as Grand Canyon, Yosemite, and Yellowstone receive at least 10 times that number. The modest attendance, combined with the fact that it is the sixth-largest park in the **contiguous** U.S., means that Big Bend is among the least crowded parks in the nation.

The lack of tourists can be attributed to two main factors. First is the park's remote location. The nearest large city, San Antonio, is six hours away, and other urban areas in the southern U.S. have closer park options. The second deterrent is the heat. Summer temperatures can be not only uncomfortable but also dangerous. As such, these typical vacation months are the slowest in the park, while the winter and spring are most popular.

About half of Big Bend's visitors stay for at least one night in the park. Those who keep their trips short often take in the sights from the roadways. More than 100 miles (161 km) of paved roads meander through the park and lead motorists to scenic overlooks, historical landmarks, and visitor facilities that provide informative exhibits. The most popular routes are the Chisos Basin Road and the Ross Maxwell Scenic Drive. The six-mile (9.7-km) Chisos Basin Road is an old CCC route that winds into the Chisos Mountains. At the road's end is a visitor center, lodge, campground, restaurant, convenience store, and numerous **trailheads**.

The Ross Maxwell Scenic Drive covers 30 miles (48.3 km) and highlights both natural and historical landmarks in the western section of the park. The natural features include the Mule Ears formation and the steep Santa Elena Canyon along the Rio Grande. Overlooks such as Sotol Vista allow guests to take in broad views of the desert landscape, while the Sam Neil Ranch and Homer Wilson Ranch offer glimpses of what Big Bend was like in the early 1900s. The Castolon area also exhibits old buildings and machines in addition to a modern visitor center, store, and campground.

Another noteworthy drive connects Panther Junction—the park headquarters—to Rio Grande Village in the southeast corner of the park. Both sites have visitor centers, stores, and gas stations, and Rio Grande Village also features a campground and picnic area. Short nature trails in the area offer excellent bird-watching. The remaining paved roads throughout Big Bend are not as packed with specific attractions, but they still offer impressive mountain and desert scenery and a few roadside stops, including exhibits about fossils and wildlife.

Unpaved roads lead to additional trailheads and points of interest. The most heavily used is the two-mile (3.2 km) jaunt that begins near Rio Grande Village and ends near the site of Langford's former hot springs resort. Only the foundation of his old bathhouse remains, but

the springs are still active and open to tourist use. Primitive roads lead to historic sites such as Glenn Springs and Mariscal Mine, but high-clearance 4x4 vehicles may be needed to reach them.

Mountain bikers may want to take on the rugged roads as well, and bicycles are permitted on roads throughout the park. Along with biking, hiking can provide a more intimate, sensory experience. Those who explore the park outside a vehicle can truly appreciate the desert silence, songbird choruses, forest whispers, and rivers' peaceful whooshing.

Most of the mountainous hikes begin near the Chisos Basin visitor area. The easiest is a paved 0.3-mile (0.5 - km) stroll called the Window View Trail, which provides impressive westward views of the surrounding mountains and The Window—a break in the mountains through which the setting sun often shines. Lost Mine Trail is an intermediate option that passes through the forests before opening up to vantage points above Pine Canyon and the distant Sierra del Carmen

PARK 7 FACTS

Keeping Your Cool

Big Bend temperatures can exceed 110 °F (43.3 °C) during the summer. Risks to hikers at this time range from sunburns to cramping to fatal heatstroke. Summer visitors should limit their outings to cooler mornings and evenings and/or higher elevations. Beyond that, having proper attire and supplies is critical. Water is of the utmost importance, and consuming a quart (0.9 liters) per hour of hiking is advised. Loose-fitting long-sleeved shirts and pants are more comfortable in the desert heat than clothes that bare more skin. Wide-brimmed hats with breathable vents protect the face, ears, and neck without trapping heat, and backpacking umbrellas allow hikers to take shade wherever they go.

range. Longer, more grueling routes lead to Emory Peak and South Rim—high points in the park that offer unmatched views of the desert and canyons below.

The terrain of desert hikes varies from barren rock formations to natural spring oases. Among the easiest is the 0.5 mile (0.8 km) Chihuahuan Desert Nature Trail. It begins at the Dugout Wells area along the road to Rio Grande Village and features stands of cottonwood trees that are home to various birds. The area also has old schoolhouse ruins. The Chimneys Trail off the Ross Maxwell Scenic Drive offers a more desert-like experience with its rugged terrain and various cacti. Indian petroglyphs, or rock carvings, can also be seen on some of the larger rock formations.

Hikes along the Rio Grande include Santa Elena Canyon Trail and Rio Grande Village Nature Trail. The former begins at the end of the

ABOVE: *If a tent has been left standing awhile, it should be checked inside and out for intruders that may have been drawn to its shade.*

Montezuma quail

Ross Maxwell road and follows along the upper rim of the canyon before descending to the river's edge. The latter lacks the elevation changes but features a spring-fed wetland that attracts many bird species.

Aside from groomed trails, hikers are permitted to go cross-country throughout most of the park. Horseback riders also have this freedom—as long as they stay off paved roadways and hiking trails. Regardless of location, hikers, bikers, and horseback riders wanting to see wildlife generally have the best luck in the early morning or later evening, since most animals rest during the midday heat.

Designated campsites and open camp zones in the **backcountry** and along primitive roads are scattered throughout the park for active visitors who want to extend their treks or seek isolation out in nature. Open fires are not permitted, but fuel stoves generally are. Water sources are unreliable and often unfit for drinking, so fluids must be brought in. Storage boxes are provided at backcountry campsites to prevent bears, javelinas, or other foraging animals from raiding human food supplies.

Travel on the Rio Grande is a popular Big Bend activity, and concessionaires offer rental equipment and shuttle services as well as guided float trips that can last a few hours to multiple days. The longer excursions involve shoreline camping. Fishing in Big Bend requires no license—only a free permit obtained from a visitor center. Angling is not especially popular, though, because only catfish are caught, and success is hit-and-miss. Swimming in the Rio Grande is discouraged because of multiple health risks, and entering backcountry springs is prohibited.

After the sun sets on Big Bend, stargazing becomes the predominant activity. The park is known for having some of the clearest night skies in the U.S., thanks to limited artificial lighting in the remote region, a dry atmosphere, and minimal air pollution. Visitors tend to see far more stars and **meteors** in Big Bend than they would ever see at home. Moonless nights in winter provide optimal conditions for stargazing.

Overnight guests can turn in at one of three campgrounds, stay at the Chisos Mountains Lodge, or camp at any of the various primitive road/ backcountry sites. Cottonwood Campground near Castolon offers 22 sites, while Chisos Basin has 56 and Rio Grande Village has 93. The latter two offer modern restrooms and a dump station for RVs. Cottonwood has outhouse-type toilets and no dump station. Rio Grande Village also has shower facilities nearby. All sites include picnic tables and grills (woodfires not being permitted). The Chisos Mountains Lodge was constructed by the CCC and has been expanded to offer a combined 72 lodging options, hotel- and motel-style rooms to stone cottages.

Big Bend has always been a place of change. Rocks and fossils tell a story of changing landscapes and ecosystems, while artifacts, ruins, and written history tell of the different people who occupied the land and the various purposes they found for it. For better or worse, plant and animal life have taken hold, disappeared, and sometimes returned to Big Bend. The sum total of such change is a region that is full of surprises and oddities begging to be explored in detail. The preservation of Big Bend as a national park has ensured that such exploration will be able to continue for many years to come.

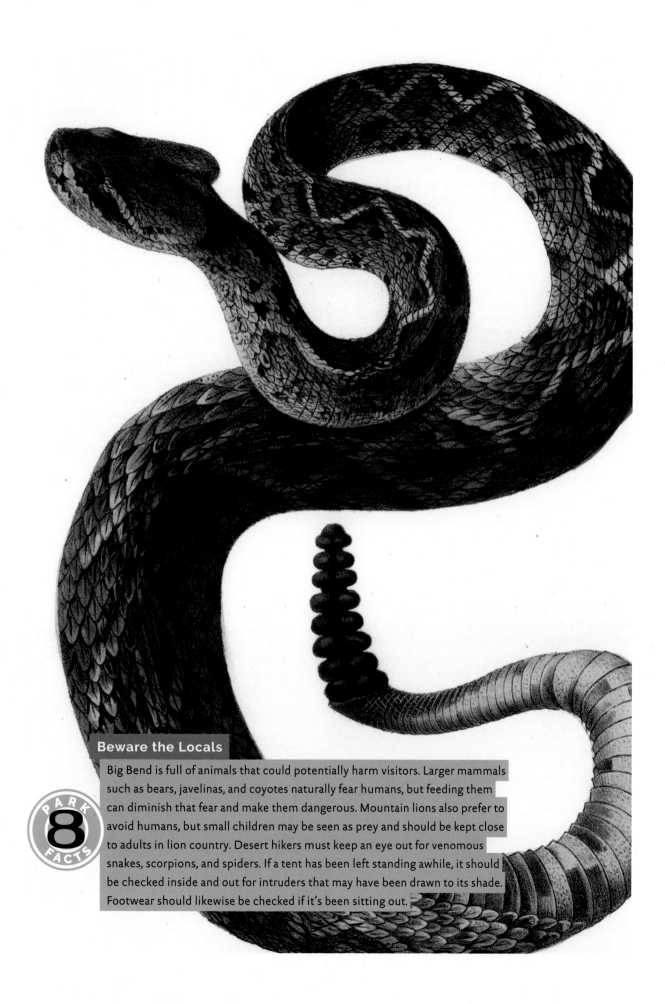

Beware the Locals

Big Bend is full of animals that could potentially harm visitors. Larger mammals such as bears, javelinas, and coyotes naturally fear humans, but feeding them can diminish that fear and make them dangerous. Mountain lions also prefer to avoid humans, but small children may be seen as prey and should be kept close to adults in lion country. Desert hikers must keep an eye out for venomous snakes, scorpions, and spiders. If a tent has been left standing awhile, it should be checked inside and out for intruders that may have been drawn to its shade. Footwear should likewise be checked if it's been sitting out.

PARK
8
FACTS

Glossary

arid: lacking enough water for things to grow; dry and barren

backcountry: an area that is away from developed or populated areas

concessionaires: people or organizations operating businesses on sites owned by someone else

contiguous: in physical contact; in the United States, contiguous states are all those except Alaska and Hawaii

ecosystems: communities of animals, plants, and other living things interacting together within an environment

erosion: wearing away by the action of natural forces such as water, wind, or ice

igneous: describing rock that formed when magma within the earth cooled and solidified

invasive: when describing plants, tending to spread harmfully, overtaking native species

meteors: pieces of space rock that, when they enter Earth's atmosphere, look like streaks of light

microbes: microscopic organisms, especially those that transmit disease

New World: the lands of North and South America, plus surrounding islands, so named because they were new to European explorers

nomadic: describing people who move frequently to new locations in order to obtain food, water, and shelter

raptors: birds of prey such as hawks, owls, eagles, and vultures

sedimentary rock: a type of rock formed by compressed sand, mud, or seashell deposits

succulents: plants with thick fleshy leaves and stems that can store water

tectonic: relating to the shifting, colliding, and separating of enormous slabs of the earth's crust

trailheads: the starting points of walking or hiking trails

tributaries: streams or rivers that connect to a larger river

Selected Bibliography

Clark, Gary. *Enjoying Big Bend National Park: A Friendly Guide to Adventures for Everyone*. College Station: Texas A&M University Press, 2023.

Laine, Don, Barbara Laine, Jack Olson, Eric Peterson, and Shane Christensen. *Frommer's National Parks of the American West*. Hoboken, N.J.: Wiley, 2012.

National Geographic Guide to the National Parks of the United States. Washington, D.C.: National Geographic, 2021.

Schullery, Paul. *America's National Parks: The Spectacular Forces That Shaped Our Treasured Lands*. New York: DK, 2001.

Tyler, Ron C. *The Big Bend: A History of the Last Texas Frontier*. College Station: Texas A&M University Press, 1996.

White, Mel. *Complete National Parks of the United States, 2nd Edition*. Washington, D.C.: National Geographic, 2016.

Websites

Big Bend National Park.
http://www.nps.gov/bibe/index.htm The official National Park Service site for Big Bend is the most complete online source for information on the park and includes tips for park sightseeing, activities, and safety. Park regulations, lodging information, and various maps are also provided.

National Geographic: Big Bend National Park.
https://www.nationalgeographic.com/travel/national-parks/article/big-bend-activities This site provides a concise visitor's guide to Big Bend, complete with photos, sightseeing suggestions, and links to other popular national parks.

Note: Every effort has been made to ensure that the websites listed above are suitable for children, that they have educational value, and that they contain no inappropriate material. However, because of the nature of the Internet, it is impossible to guarantee that these sites will remain active indefinitely or that their contents will not be altered.